CHOOSING THE RIGHT WAY

Share Christ with Muslims

Revised Edition

EMMANUEL ASANTE

Zeta Publishing

Ocala, FL

Zeta Publishing, Inc
3850 SE 58th Ave
Ocala, FL 34480
www.zetapublishing.com

Ordering Information:
Quantity sales. Special discounts are available on quantity purchases by corporations, associations, and others. For details, contact the publisher at the address above.
Orders by U.S. trade bookstores and wholesalers. Please contact Zeta Publishing: Tel: (352) 694-2553; Fax: (352) 694-1791 or visit www.zetapublishing.com

First published by Trafford in 2012

Rev. Date: 8/12/2017

ISBN: 978-1-947191-32-7 (sc)

ISBN: 978-1-947191-33-4 (e)

Library of Congress Control Number: 2017952546

Printed in the United States of America

Table of Contents

Dedication

I would like to dedicate this book to the glory of God who gave me the strength to accomplish my vision.

I would like also to dedicate this book to my wife, Gina and my three children, Linda, Rita, and Isaac Asante who encouraged me during the time of frustration while working on my manuscript.

I am also indebted to dedicate this to Dr. Rockeybell Adatura, Mr. Emmanuel Abbey of the University of Ghana [Department of Religion], Miss Wendy De Youngster, Dr. and Mrs. Somuah, Mr. Emmanuel Nanor, Mr. William Dorgbadzi and to all who backed me with prayers to bring this to light.

Introduction

Sometimes people of other religions begin to doubt the deity and the plain truths about Jesus Christ and, for that matter, ignore God's plan of salvation. The aim of this religious book is to make known the authenticity of Christianity and also to show the true way of Jehovah God. This religious book has some scriptural references concerning Jesus Christ from the Holy Bible and the Glorious Qur'an that testify to these facts. Again, these facts have been outlined in a compare-and-contrast manner so that anyone could understand and make references easier from the Holy Bible and the Glorious Qur'an.

There is a perception among people from the other religions that the kingdom of God is like a sports stadium that consists of many entrances where one could get easy access to the stadium through any of the gates. In other words, one could gain salvation by passing through any other medium in order to get to Heaven. In a sharp contrast, the Word of God debunks that notion, as it is written, "For God so loved the world that He gave his only begotten son and that whosoever believes in him should not perish but have everlasting life" (John 3:16 KJV). In other words, "whosoever shall call upon the name of the Lord shall be saved" (Rom. 10:13). Jesus Himself also declared and said, "I am the way, the truth and the life, no one comes to the Father except (through) me" (John 14:6 NIV).

Again, Jesus said, "Yes, I am the gate. Those who comes in through me will be saved" (John 10:9a NIV). These powerful declarations made by the Lord Jesus Christ gives clear indication that "neither is there salvation in any other, for there is none under Heaven given among men, whereby we must be saved" (Acts 4:12 KJV) but through the name of Jesus Christ. There was no master who ever lived on this planet Earth who was able to make such a powerful declaration apart from the Lord Jesus Christ. All those who are seeking God through any other path are doing so in their own damnation.

Having established the above fact, it is therefore imperative to direct our attention on what the sacred writings of Islam have to say about salvation. The Qur'an, on it's own way of salvation, states that "the weighing on that day is the true (weighing). As for those whose scales are heavy, they are the successful. As those whose scales are light, they are those who lose their soul because they disbelieved Our revelations" (Sura 7, Al-A'raf 8-9).

The above Qur'anic verse means that if your good deeds outweigh your bad deeds, then you qualify to go to Paradise after life here on this earth. According to a theologian named John L. Esposito, a university professor of religion, the author of the Unholy War and What Everyone Needs to Know about Islam, quoted from the Qur'an, which states, "Then those whose balance of good deeds is heavy will attain salvation, but those whose balance are light will have lost their souls and abide in Hell forever" (Qur'an 23:102-103). John Esposito commented on the above Qur'anic verse, "Qur'an's vision of the afterlife is both spiritual and physical. Bodies and souls will be joined and pleasures of heavenly gardens of bliss and the pain of hellfire will be fully experienced." He further stressed, "On the Day of

Judgement, a great cataclysmic cosmic event that will occur at a moment known only to God, all will be raised from the dead." God will judge each person by the standards brought by the person's community's prophets and scripture, using the record of each person's actions throughout his or her life are recorded in the Book of Deeds." He therefore quoted another verse from the Qur'an to affirm his claims, which states, "Those who believe and do righteous deeds they are the best creatures. Their reward is with their Lord; Gardens of Paradise beneath which rivers flow. They will dwell therein forever. God well-pleased with them and they with him. This is for those who hold their Lord in awe" (Qur'an 98:7-8).

However, the Islamic view point of salvation demands the impossibility of an individual. It is like asking a lame man to walk, which is impossible. How will you know for sure whether you have become good enough to get to Heaven? What's more? There are no scoreboards that will tally scores in your life for you to take note. Being saved through your good deeds means you need to know what good deeds and bad deeds are. We could be doing something we think is good when in fact it is not. There are also mistakes in life, and how can you draw the bottom line? That is why the apostle Paul said, "There is no one righteous, not even one seeks God. All have turned away, they have together become worthless, there is no one who is good, not even one" (Rom. 3:10-13).

Furthermore, if God is going to keep scores in our lives, shouldn't He at least tell us the rules of the game? If that be the case, then the set of rules that defines what is good and bad is enshrined in the Holy Bible. The Word of God teaches us that "whosoever keeps the whole law and stumbles at just one point is guilty of breaking all of it." [James 2:10] The fundamentals of those rules are the Ten Commandments, and therefore, the problem is none of us have perfectly obeyed God's rules, for the Word of God reminds us, "For who said: Do not commit adultery also said do not murder. If you do not commit adultery but do commit murder, you have become a law breaker" (James 2:11).

Jehovah God has given us the rules, but we have broken it. This means that God considers you as a lawbreaker. Consequently, there must be a way out so that the individual can gain salvation without much difficulty. God has therefore given us the second chance to accept His free gift, who is Jesus Christ, so that we may have everlasting life. Graciously, it is by the grace of God that we are saved and not by our good works, as it is written, "For it is by Grace you have been saved through faith and not from yourselves, it is the gift of God so that no one can boast" (Eph. 2:8-9 KJV). Apparently, Jehovah God has made a provision for salvation through the redemptive work of Christ on the cross at Calvary so that mankind would be justified through the blood of Jesus. Obviously, that is the perfect atonement God has provided for humanity, for it is written, "And being found in a fashion as a man he humbled himself and became obedient on to death even death on the cross. Wherefore God has highly exalted him and given him a name which is above every name, at the name of Jesus every knee should bow of things in Heaven, things in earth and things under earth and every tongue should confess that Jesus Christ is Lord to the glory of God the Father" (Phil. 2:8-9 KJV).

Precious one, I wish you will not find it difficult to accept the idea of redemption because it depends on Christ's shameful death on the cross.

Books used for references are
The Holy Bible (KJV, NIV, Good News) and the Glorious Qu'ran (English translation by Mahmud Y. Zayid [Dar Al-Choura] and also by Marmaduke Pickthall).

The Angel Gabriel Announces the Glad Tidings to Mary

The angel Gabriel is a messenger of God who delivers special messages to humanity. Again, Christians of the orthodox faith always refer to Angel Gabriel as the Archangel of God. The Qur'an also acknowledges the angel Gabriel (as a medium through which the Qur'an was revealed to the prophet Mohammed (p.b.u.h.). On the other hand, such claims were not recorded anywhere in the Bible. However, both the Bible and the Qur'an confirm that the angel Gabriel was truly sent by God to deliver a special message to Mary regarding the birth of Jesus Christ, for it is revealed in the Qur'an,

"The Angel said to Mariam (Mary): "Allah bids you rejoice in a Word from Him. His name is Al-Masih (Messiah), Isa (Jesus), the son of Mariam (Mary). He shall be noble in this world in the next, and shall be favored by Allah. (Sura 3, Al-Imran 45)

Again, another confirmation from the Sura records,

"Lord," she said, "how can I bear a child when no man has touched me?" He replied, "Such is the Will of Allah. He creates whom He will. When He decrees a thing, He needs only say 'Be,' and it is." (Sura 3, Al-Imran 47)

These two verses from the Qur'an have confirmed beyond any reasonable doubt that the angel Gabriel was really sent by God in order to announce the glad tidings to Mary. The angel further said that the child shall be called Jesus, the Messiah. It further stressed that when God decrees a thing, "He needs only say 'Be' and it is," and it sounds like a Christian doctrine. When God wants to create a thing, He only needs to speak the Word and it comes into existence. For instance, God said, "Let there be light," and there was light (Gen. 1:3).

Now let's direct our attention to the Gospel, for it is written,

> Now in the sixth month the angel Gabriel was sent by God to a city of Galilee named Nazareth, to a virgin betrothed to a man whose name was Joseph, of the house of David. The virgin's name was Mary. And having come in, the angel said to her, "Rejoice, highly favored one, the Lord is with you; blessed are you among women." But when she saw him, she was troubled at his saying, and considered what manner of greeting this was. Then the angel said, "Do not be afraid, Mary, for you have found favor with God. And behold you will conceive in your womb and bring forth a son, and shall call His name Jesus. He will be great, and will be called the son of the Highest; and the Lord God will give Him a throne of His father David. And He will reign over the house of Jacob forever, and of His Kingdom there will be no end." Then Mary said to the angel, "How can this be, since I do not know a man?" And the angel answered and said to her, "The Holy Spirit will come upon you, and the power of the Highest will overshadow you; therefore,

also, that Holy One who is to be born will be called the Son of God. Now indeed, Elizabeth your relative has also conceived a son in her old age; and this is now the sixth month of her who is called barren. For with God nothing will be impossible." Then Mary said, "Behold the maidservant of the Lord! Let it be to me according to your word." And the angel departed from her. (Luke 1:26-38)

The angel Gabriel also visited a Galilee priest called Zechariah in the temple and announced to him that his barren wife, Elizabeth, would give birth to a child. This child shall be called John the Baptist, who shall prepare the way for the Lord Jesus Christ.

It came to pass that after His mother Mary was betrothed to Joseph before they came together, she was found with a child of the Holy Spirit. Then Joseph her husband, being a just man and not wanting to make her a public example, was minded to put her away secretly. But while he thought about these things, behold, an angel of the Lord appeared to him in a dream, saying "Joseph, son of David, do not be afraid to take to you Mary your wife, for that which is conceived in her is of the Holy Spirit. And she will bring forth a son, and you shall call His name Jesus, for He will save his people from their sins." Now all this was done that it might be fulfilled, which was spoken by the Lord through the prophet saying, "Behold, a virgin shall be with child, and bear a son, and they shall call His name Immanuel, which is translated God with us." Then Joseph, being aroused from sleep, did as the angel of the Lord commanded him, and he took his wife, and did not know her till she had brought forth his first Son. And he called his name Jesus. (Matt. 1;18-25)

Dear reader, you will realize that there was a divine intervention by an angel of God who visited Joseph during his sleep and disclosed the whole truth to him. Joseph became convinced of the greatest honor God had bestowed on both of them and so decided to wed his wife, Mary, rather than to put her away.

What is more? Jesus's name is special, from Heaven, which the angel Gabriel gave to Mary to name her Child. Why can't you also believe in that name, especially if you are an unbeliever?

The Unique Birth of Christ

The birth of Christ has become the most well-known religious story of history, and it is being observed throughout the world during Christmas season. Christians believe that Jesus was born of the Virgin Mary and that He is the incarnation of God as God the Son.

The Glorious Qur'an has its own translation of the birth of Christ. The Sura records, "The Angel said to Mariam (Mary): "Allah bids you rejoice in a Word from Him. His name is Al-Masih (Messiah), Isa (Jesus), the son of Mariam (Mary). He shall be noble in this World and in the next, and shall be favored by Allah. He shall speak to men in His Cradle and in the prime of manhood, and shall lead a righteous life" (Sura 3, Al-Imran 45-46).

The above Qur'anic verse has given clear indication that Jesus Christ was born of the Virgin Mary after the angel had announced the glad tidings to her. The birth of Christ, as described by the Qur'an, is quite unfamiliar to the Christians. Joseph, the magi, and the shepherds were not mentioned, so the details in connection to the birth of Christ in the Qur'an cannot be reconciled with the New Testament records. The scripture only agrees with the Qur'an on the "Son of Mariam (Mary)" as it is written in Mark 6:3, which states, "Is this not the carpenter's son of Mary?" The scripture has the authentic record of the birth of Christ, so let us direct our attention to the Gospel, which states,

In those days a decree went out from Caesar Augustus that all World should be registered. So all of them went into their home-towns to be registered. Joseph also went up from Galilee, out of the city of Nazareth, into Judea, to the city of David, which is called Bethlehem, because he was of the house and lineage of David, to be registered with Mary, his betrothed wife, And it came to pass that the days were completed for her to deliver. And she brought forth her firstborn son, and wrapped Him in swaddling clothes, and laid Him in a manger, because there was no room for them in the inn. (Luke 2:1-7)

The birth of Christ was characterized by many heavenly events. As soon the angel finished his announcement to the shepherds about the glad tidings, an army of angels appeared to confirm it by singing to the glory of God, for the Word of God tells us,

Now there were in the same country shepherds living out in the fields, keeping watch over their flock by night. And behold, an angel of the Lord stood before them, and they were greatly afraid. Then the angel said to them, "Do not be afraid, for behold, I bring you glad tidings of great joy which will be to all people. For there is born to you this day in the city of David a Savior, who is Christ the Lord. And this will be a sign to you: You will find the Baby wrapped in swaddling clothes, lying in a manger." And suddenly there was with the angel a multitude of Heavenly host praising God and saying: Glory to God in the highest, and on earth peace, good-will toward men.

So it was, when the angels had gone away from them into Heaven, the shepherds said to one another, "Let us now go to Bethlehem and see this thing that has come to pass. When the

Lord has made known to us." And they came with haste and found Mary and Joseph, and the Baby lying in a manger.

Now when they had seen Him, they made widely known the saying which was told them concerning this child. And all those who heard it marveled at those things which were told them by the shepherds. But Mary kept all these things and pondered them in her heart. Then the shepherds returned, glorifying and praising God for all the things that they had heard and seen, as it had been told them. (Luke 2:8-20)

When the angel announced the glad tidings to the shepherds, the glory of God shone around them, and they were afraid, but the angel told them, "Don't be afraid, but behold, I bring you glad tidings of great joy. For there is born to you this day in the city of David a Savior." He explained to them that this Savior was from the city of David; therefore, he was one of David's descendants. He was also the long-awaited Messiah and Lord.

And when eight days were completed for the circumcision of the child. His name was called Jesus, the name given by the angel before he was conceived in the womb. Now when the days of her purification according to the law of Lord (as it is written in the Law of the Lord, "Every male who opens the womb shall be called holy to the Lord"), and to offer a sacrifice according to what is said in the Law of the Lord. (Luke 2:21-24)

And behold, there was a man in Jerusalem whose name was Simeon, and this man was just and devout, waiting for the Consolation of Israel, and the Holy Spirit was upon him, and it had been revealed to him by the Holy Spirit that he would not see death before he had seen the Lord Jesus Christ. So he came by the Spirit into the temple. And when the parents brought the child Jesus to do for him according to the custom of the law, he took him up in his arms and blessed God and said, "Lord, now you are letting your servant depart in peace according to your Word, for my eyes have seen your salvation which you have prepared before the face of all people a light to bring revelation to the Gentiles, and the glory of your people Israel."

And Joseph and His mother marveled at those things which were spoken of Him. Then Simeon blessed them, and said to Mary His mother, "Behold, this Child is destined for the fall and rise of many in Israel, and for a sign which will be spoken against (yes, a sword will pierce through your own soul also), that the thoughts of many hearts may be revealed." (Luke 2:25-35)

It came to pass, after Simeon had spoken, the old prophetess Anna also came forward to praise the Lord, for St. Luke states, "Now there was one Anna, a prophetess, the daughter of Phanuel, of the tribe of Asher: she was of a great age, and had lived with her husband seven years from her virginity; and this woman was a widow of about eighty-four years, who did not depart from the temple, but served God with fastings and prayers night and day. And coming in that instant she gave thanks to the Lord, and spoke of Him to all those who looked for redemption in Jerusalem" (Luke 2:36-38).

Furthermore, after this visit to the temple, the family of three returned to Bethlehem, the city of their forefathers. By that time, the crowd that came for the census had left, and so they were able to find a more suitable place to live than with the animals.

Finally, the Gospel states that three wise men from the East were led by a star and came to Bethlehem to worship the infant Christ. Why can't you also give your life to Him and worship Him?

John the Baptist Prepares the Way

John the Baptist began his ministry preaching by saying, "Prepare the way of the Lord and make His paths straight. He has a burning awareness of who was to come before him who would baptize in fire and Spirit" (Matt. 1:78).

It is just amazing how the Qur'an also acknowledges John the Baptist as a righteous man who came to pave the way for Jesus Christ, for the Sura declares,

> "Then Zechariah prayed unto his Lord and said, "My Lord, Bestow me of thy bounty offspring. Lo! Thou art the Hearer of Prayer."

> And the angels called to him as he stood praying in the Sanctuary: Allah sweth thee glad tiding of (a son whose name is) John (who cometh) to confirm a Word from Allah, lordly, chaste, a prophet of the righteous.

(Sura 3, Al-Imran 38-39)

Although the above Qur'anic text did not mention Elizabeth's name, there were similarities that support the vivid account of the scriptures concerning John the Baptist, which records "In the days of Herod, king of Judea there was a priest named Zachariah of the division of Abijah; and he had a wife of the daughters of Aaron, and her name was Elizabeth. And they were both righteous before God, walking in all the commandments and ordinances of the Lord blameless. But they had no child, because Elizabeth was barren and both were advanced in years. Now while he was serving as priest before God when his division was on duty, according to the custom of the priesthood, it felt to him by lot to enter the temple of the Lord and burn incense. And the whole multitude of the people was praying outside at the hour of incense. And there appeared to him an angel of the Lord standing on the right side of the Altar of incense. And Zechariah was troubled when he saw him, and fear fell upon him. But the angel said to him, 'Do not be afraid, Zechariah for your prayer is heard and your wife Elizabeth will bear you a son, and you shall call his name John.'" (Luke 1: 5-13)

And Zechariah said to the angel, "How shall I know this? For I am an old man, and my wife is advanced in years." And the angel answered him, "I am Gabriel, who stand in the presence of God; and I was sent to speak to you, and to bring you this good news. And behold, you will be silent and unable to speak until the day that these things come to pass, because you did not believe my words, which will be fulfilled in their time". And the people were waiting for Zechariah and they wondered at his delay in the temple. And when he came out he could not speak to them and they perceived that he had seen a vision in the temple, and he made signs to them and remained dumb. And when his time of service was ended he went to his home. After these days his wife Elizabeth conceived, and for five months she hid herself, saying, "thus the Lord has done to me in the days when he looked on me, to take away my reproach among men." (Luke 1 18-25)

"In those days Mary arose and went with haste into the hill country to the city of Judah, and she entered the house of Zachariah and greeted Elizabeth and when Elizabeth heard the greeting of Mary the baby leaped in her womb, and Elizabeth was filled with the Holy Spirit." (Luke 1:39-41)

Now the time came for Elizabeth to be delivered, and she gave birth to a son. And her neighbors and kinsfolk heard that the Lord had shown great mercy to her and they rejoiced with her. And on the eighth day they came to circumcise the child; and they would have named John Zachariah after his father, but his mother said "Not so, he shall be called John." And they said to her none of your kindred is called by this name. And they made signs to his father inquiring what he would have him called. And he asked for a writing tablet and wrote, "His name is John." And they all marveled. "And immediately his mouth was opened and his tongue loosed, and he spoke, blessing God. And fear came on all their neighbors. And all these things were talked about through all the hill country of Judea and all who heard them laid them up in their hearts, saying, what then will this child be?" For the hand of the Lord was with him. (Luke 1:57-66)

In the fullness of time, there was a man sent from God whose name was John. He came preaching in the wilderness of Judea and saying, "Repent, for the Kingdom of Heaven is at hand," for this is He who was spoken of by the prophet Isaiah, saying, "The voice of one crying in the wilderness, prepare the way of the Lord, make his paths straight." And John himself was clothed in camel's hair, with a leather belt around his waist, and his food was locusts and wild honey. Then Jerusalem, all Judea, and all the region around Jordan went out to him and were baptized by him in the river Jordan, confessing their sins.

But when he saw many of the Pharisees and Sadducees

coming to his baptism, he said to them, "Brood of vipers, who has warned you to flee from the wrath to come? Therefore bear fruits worthy of repentance and do not say to yourselves we have Abraham as our Father. For I say unto you that God is able to raise up children to Abraham from these stones. And even now the axe is laid to the root of the trees. Therefore every tree which does not bear good fruits is cut down and thrown into the fire. I indeed baptized you with water unto repentance but He who is coming after me is mightier than I, whose sandals I am not worthy to carry. He will baptize you with the Holy Spirit and with fire. His winnowing fan is in his hands and He will thoroughly purge His threshing floor, and gather His wheat into the ban, but He will burn up the chaff with unquenchable fire." (Matt. 3:1-12)

John the Baptist, who came to prepare the way for Christ's appearance, was foretold by the prophets in the Old Testament of the Bible. The rank of John the Baptist was determined by the chain of miracles that accompanied his birth and the powerful message that he gave.

Years passed, a man came to live in the wilderness, a prophet called John the Baptist. The people of Jerusalem and all Judea came to him to be baptized, to be washed in the waters of the river Jordan as they confessed their sins.

John told them, "Someone will come who is much greater than I. I baptize you in water, but he will baptize you in Holy Spirit." One day Jesus himself came to be baptized by John. When Jesus left the water, he saw the heaven opened, and the Spirit of God descended upon him like a dove. From heaven came a voice, saying, "This is my beloved Son, in whom I am well pleased" (Matt. 3:17).

And it came to pass that the next day when John saw Jesus coming toward him, he said, "Look at the Lamb of God who takes away the sin of the world. This is the one of whom I said, a man who comes after me has surpassed me because he was before me. I myself did not know him, but the reason I came to baptize with water was that he might be revealed to Israel."

Then John gave this testimony: "I saw the Spirit come down from Heaven as a dove and remain on Him. I would not have known Him, except that the One who sent me to baptize with water told me the man on whom you will see the Spirit came down and remain is He who will baptize with the Holy Spirit I have seen and testified that this is the Son of God" (John 1:29-34).

Dear reader, I want to encourage you to ponder over the pronouncement made by John the Baptist "Behold the Lamb of God who takes away the sin of the World" very critically and to make the right decision now simply because Jesus was the final and the best atonement God provided for mankind.

The Miracle Life of Jesus

There were so many supernatural deeds by Jesus Christ that were not recorded in the Bible because there would not be any room to contain it. The Gospel of John states, "Jesus did other things as well if everyone of them were written, even the whole world would not have room for the books that would be written" (John 21:25). In the Christian faith, Jesus's miracles were a vehicle for His message to the world, and it is amazing how the Qur'an could also carry out that message to the world, for it is written in the Sura, which reveals,

"Lord," she said, "how can I bear a child when no man has touched me?"

He replied, "Such is the will of Allah, He creates whom he will. When he decrees a thing, He needs only say 'Be,' and it is. He will instruct him in the Book and in wisdom, in the Torah (Old Testament) and in the Gospel, and send him forth as an apostle to the children of Israel. He will say, "I bring you a sign from your Lord. From Clay, I will make for you the likeness of a bird. I shall breathe into it and, by Allah's leave, it shall become a living bird. By Allah's leave, I shall give sight to the blind man, heal the leper, and raise the dead to life." (Sura 3, Al-Imran 47-49)

The above declarations are all quotations from the Qur'an. The first and second verses were the conversation between the Virgin Mary and the angel who announced the glad tidings. It is very amazing how some of these Qur'anic verses sound just like a Christian doctrine, especially the last verse, which states, "I shall give sight to the blind man, heal the leper, and raise the dead to life."

This last verse refers to the Lord Jesus Christ, who came to save the lost, heal the sick, cleanse the leper, cast out demons, and raise the dead back to life, as it is written, "He sent His Word and healed them and delivered them from their destructions" (Psalm 107:20).

Again, the Acts of the apostle states, "How God anointed Jesus of Nazareth with the Holy Ghost and with power; who went about doing good, and healing all that were oppressed of the devil; for the God with Him" (Acts 10:38).

The Bible records that Jesus came from Galilee to Jordan to be baptized by John. But John tried to deter him, saying, "I need to be baptized by you." Jesus said, "Let it be so now, it is proper for us to do this to fulfill all righteousness." Then John consented.

As soon as Jesus was baptized, he went out of the water. At that moment, heaven was opened, and he saw the Spirit of God descending like a dove and lightning on him. And a voice came from Heaven, saying, "This is my beloved Son, in whom I am well pleased" (Matt. 3:13-17).

And Jesus being full of the Holy Ghost returned from Jordan and was led by the Spirit into the wilderness to be tempted by the devil. And when He had fasted forty nights, He was hungry. Now when the devil came to Him, he said, "If you are the Son of God, command that these stones become bread." But he answered and said, "It is written, man shall not live by bread alone, but by every word that proceeds from the mouth of God." (Matt. 4:1-4)

Then the devil took Him up into the holy city, set Him on the pinnacle of the temple, and said to Him, "If you are the Son of God, throw yourself down, for it is written, He shall give His angels charge concerning you, and in their hands they shall bear you up, lest you dash your foot against a stone." Jesus said to him, "It is written again, You shall not tempt the Lord your God." (Matt. 4:5-7)

Again, the devil took Him up on an exceedingly high mountain, and showed Him all the kingdoms of the world and their glory. And he said to Him, "All these things I will give you if you will fall down and worship me." Then Jesus said to him, "Away with you, Satan! For it is written, You shall worship the Lord your God and Him only you shall serve." Then the devil left him, and behold, angels came and ministered to him. (Matt. 4:8-11)

After Jesus returned from the wilderness where He had faced and defeated Satan, He returned in the power of the Spirit into Galilee (Luke 4:14). On the Sabbath day, he came to his hometown, Nazareth, went into the synagogue, and with all eyes fixed on him, openly declared the ministry God had given him to fulfill. Jesus opened the Book of Isaiah and began to read, "The Spirit of the Lord is upon me, because he has anointed me to preach the gospel to the poor; he has sent me to heal the brokenhearted, to preach deliverance to the captives, and recovery of sight to the blind, and to set at liberty them that are bound. To preach the acceptable year of the Lord" (Luke 4:18-19).

Then Jesus closed the book and sat down. With all eyes fixed on him, anxiously waiting and wondering what he would say next, Jesus said, "This day is this scripture fulfilled in your ears" (Luke 4:20-21).

After this, Jesus healed the blind, cleansed the leper, cast out demons, healed all manner of diseases, and raised the dead back to life. Jesus's supernatural deeds can therefore be categorized into four parts, which includes cures, exorcisms, raising the dead back to life, and control over nature. In the Gospel according John, signs and wonders were part of Jesus's ministry, such as changing water into wine and raising Lazarus back to life. Christianity is alive and real because Jehovah God is still in the working miracle business, for the Word of God reminds us that Jesus Christ is the same yesterday, today, and forever (Heb. 13:8).

Again, the Almighty God is still using Jesus's followers to heal the sick, to cast out demons, and to deliver the oppressed with the help of the Holy Spirit, as it is written, "When He ascended on high he led captives in his train and gave gifts to men" (Eph. 4:8).

Jesus said, "And these signs shall follow them that believe; in my name shall they cast out devils, they shall speak with the new tongues, they shall take up serpents; and if they drink any deadly thing, it shall not hurt them; they shall lay hands on the sick, and they shall recover" (Mark 16:17-18).

Beloved, all these promises by the Lord Jesus belongs to you also if only you will give your life to Him.

The Word Was Made Flesh and Dwelt Among Us

The Word means the revelation and expression of God, and the name of the Word made flesh on earth is called Jesus Christ. Jesus was the name Joseph was told to give the Child by the angel of the Lord because it means "Savior," for it is written "An angel of the Lord appeared to him in a dream, saying, Joseph, son of David, do not be afraid to take Mary as your wife, for the child who has been conceived in her is of the Holy Spirit. She will bear a son and you shall call His name Jesus, for He will save His people from their sin."

The Qur'an also enjoins the Bible to acknowledge the fact that Jesus Christ is the Word of God, for the Sura reveals, "Al-Masih (Messiah), Isa (Jesus), the Son of Mariam (Mary), was no more than Allah's Apostle and His Word which He cast to Mariam (Mary): a Spirit from Him" (Sura 4, Al-Nisa 171b).

The above Qur'anic verse has confirmed beyond any reasonable doubt that Jesus Christ is the Word of God and also the Messiah, which means "the anointed one." The Qur'an also supports the Bible to acknowledge Jesus Christ as the Word, which was made flesh and dwelt among us. Jesus Christ, therefore, has so many titles, such as the Messiah or Christ. Christ was referred to as the long-awaited king of the Jews who would give victory to the people and bear the government of the world on His shoulders. For it is recorded in the Book of Isaiah, which states, "For a child will be born to us, a son will be given to us, and the government will rest on His shoulders and His name will be called Wonderful, Mighty God, Eternal Father, Prince of Peace" (Isa. 9:6).

It is therefore imperative to focus our attention on the detailed account from the scriptures, which states,

> In the beginning was the Word was with God and the Word was God. The same was in the beginning with God. All things were made by Him and without Him was not anything made that was made. In Him was life, and the life was the light of men. And the light shines in darkness, and the darkness comprehended it not. There was a man sent from God whose name was John. The same came for a witness, to bear witness of the light that all men through him might believe. He was not that light but was sent to bear witness of that light. That was the true light which lightens every man that cometh into the World. He was in the World and the world was made by Him; and the World knew him not.

> He came unto his own, and his own received Him not. But as many as received Him, to them gave He power to become the sons of God, even to them that believed on his name: Which were born, not of blood, nor of the will of the flesh, nor of the will of man, but of God.

And the Word was made flesh and dwelt among us, and we beheld his glory, the glory as of the only begotten of the Father full of grace and truth. (John 1:1-14)

The Living Word (Logos) was with God before the foundations of the earth. He was one with God and was the express image of God. The Word of God portrays the clear image of who Jesus is, and therefore, Christ and the Word are inseparable—that is, what can be said about Christ can also be said about the Word. Just as Jesus, the Living Word has life in Himself, so does his Word.

Jesus Christ is the Living Word of God. In other words, Jesus is the Living Word, and the Bible is the written Word of God, as it is written, "And He was clothed with a vesture dipped in blood; and his name is called the Word of God" (Rev. 19:13).

Again, God spoke to the world through His Word, who was manifested in the flesh. The apostle Paul told the Hebrews, "In the past God spoke to our forefathers through the prophets at many times and in various ways, but in these last days He has spoken to us by His Son, whom He appointed heir of all things, and through whom He made the Universe" (Heb. 1:1-2).

Furthermore, God sent His Word to reveal His will, to redeem and reconcile man back onto himself, for the Gospel states, "But the fullness of the time was come, God sent forth His Son, made of a woman, made under the law. To redeem them that were under the law, that we might receive the adoption of Sons" (Gal. 4:4-5).

Above all, John who was one of Christ's disciples, called Jesus the Word of Life. He is both the Word and the Life, who was with God from the beginning, for the Gospel records, "That which was from the beginning, which we have heard, which we have seen with our eyes, which we have looked upon, and our hands had handled, of the Word of Life; (for the life was manifested, and we have seen it, and bear witness and show unto you that eternal life, which was with the father, and was manifested unto us); that which we have seen and heard declare we unto you" (1 John 1:1-3).

Lastly, God sent His Word (Christ, the Living Word), and He spoke forth words of eternal life, healing, deliverance, cleansing, total restoration. He confronted and defeated Satan by the powerful words coming from His mouth when He came to earth and took upon Himself a body of flesh and blood, for the Gospel reveals, "He sent His word and healed them, and delivered them from their destructions" (Psalm 107:20).

Beloved, the Bible declares, "But as many as received Him, to them gave He power to become the sons of God, even to them that believe in His name." Why can't you take advantage to become a child of God by receiving Christ as your personal savior now?

Jesus Came to FulFill the Old Testament

Jesus Christ came to fulfill the predictions of the prophets who had long foretold that a Savior would one day appear to fulfill the Old Testament. He came to fulfill the law by becoming the perfect sacrifice for sin to which all the Old Testament offerings had ever pointed. It is amazing to note how the Qur'an also supports this claim, for the Qur'an records,

After those prophets We (God) sent forth Isa (Jesus), the son of Mariam (Mary), confirming the Torah (Old Testament) already revealed, and gave him the Gospel, in which there is guidance and light, corroborating that which was revealed before it in the Torah (Old Testament), a guide and an admonition to the righteous. (Sura 5, Al-Maidah 46)

Again another Sura also states,

I come to confirm to Torah (Old Testament) that has already been revealed and to make lawful to you some of the things you are forbidden. I bring you a sign from your Lord: therefore, fear

Him and obey Me. (Sura 3, Al-Imran 50)

These two Qur'anic verses support the claims that Jesus Christ came to confirm the Old Testament. It is further explained in the second verse that it was Jesus who made that declaration, and therefore, everyone should obey Him. Jesus came to fulfill the moral law by yielding to it a perfect obedience and by paying the penalty for our breaking of it with His atoning blood, which we never could have paid.

The above established facts have therefore proved beyond reasonable doubts that it was indeed Jesus Christ who came to fulfill the law, for the Gospel reminds us what Jesus said, "Don not think that I have come to abolish them but to fulfill them" (Matt. 5:17).

Again, the scripture records, "The law was given by Moses but grace and truth came through Jesus Christ" (John 1:17).

The Gospel teaches us that no human person was able to fulfill the law, for it is written

For all who rely on works of the law are under a curse; for it is written: "Cursed be everyone who does not abide by all things written in the book of the law, and do them." Now it is evident that no man is justified before God by the law; for "He who through faith is righteous shall live" but the law does not rest on faith, for "He who does them shall live by them." Christ redeemed us from the curse of the law, having become a curse for us—for it is written, "Cursed be everyone who hangs on a tree"—that in Christ Jesus the blessing of Abraham might come upon the Gentiles, that we might receive the promise of the Spirit through faith. (Gal. 3:10-14)

The Lord Jesus came to fulfill the law for us to have our redemption through the sacrificial death on the cross at Calvary, for the scripture tells us in the Epistle to the Galatians, "But when the fullness of the time was come, God sent forth the his Son, made of a woman, made under the law, to redeem them that were under the law, that we might receive the adoption of Sons" (Gal. 4:4-5).

The apostle Paul at one time became angry with the people of Galatians for observing the law. He said to them,

You foolish Galatians. Who has bewitched you? Before your very eyes Jesus Christ was clearly portrayed as crucified. I would like to learn just one thing from you: Did you receive the Spirit by observing the Law, or believing what you heard? Are you so foolish? After beginning with the Spirit, are you now trying to attain your goal by human efforts? Have you suffered so much for nothing? If it really was for nothing. Does God give you His Spirit and work miracles among you because you observed the Law; or because you believed what you heard? Consider Abraham: He believed God, and it was credited to him as righteousness, understand, then, that those who believe are children of Abraham. The Scripture foresaw that God would justify the Gentiles by faith, and announced the Gospel in advance to Abraham: "All nation will be blessed through you." So those who have faith are blessed along with Abraham, the man of faith." (Gal. 3:1-9)

Again, the Epistle to the Romans tells us,

Therefore no one will be declared righteous in his sight by observing the law rather through the Law we became conscious of sin. But now righteousness of God, apart from law, has been known, to which the law and the prophets testify. This righteousness from God comes through faith of Jesus Christ to all who believe, there is no difference, for all have sinned and fall short of glory of God, and are justified freely by his grace through the redemption that came by Christ Jesus. (Rom. 3:20-24)

Furthermore, the Epistle to Romans states,

For what the Law was powerless to do in that it was weakened by the sinful nature, God did by sending His own son in the likeness of sinful man to be a sin offering. And so He condemned sin in sinful man in order that the righteous requirements of the law might be fully met in us, who do not live according to the sinful nature but according to the Spirit. (Rom. 8:3-4)

Finally, what can we say about the law and the promise? The Bible explicitly expresses itself on the Epistle to Galatians, which states, "Brothers, let me take an example from everyday life." Just as no one can set aside or add to a human covenant that has been duly established, so it is in this case. The promises were spoken to Abraham and his seed. The scripture does not say "and to seeds," meaning many people, but "and to your seed," meaning one person, who is Christ.

What I mean is this. The law, introduced 430 years later, does not set aside the covenant previously established by God and, thus do away with the promise. For if the inheritance depends on the law, then it no longer depends on a promise, but God in his grace gave it to Abraham through a promise.

What, then, was the purpose of the law? It was added because of transgression until the seed the promise referred to had come. The law was put into effect through angels by a mediator. A mediator, however, does not represent just one party, but God is one.

Is the law, therefore, opposed to the promise of God? Absolutely not. For if a law had been given that could impact life, then righteousness would certainly have come by the law. But the scripture declares that the whole world is a prisoner of sin so that what was promised, being given through faith in Jesus Christ, might be given to those who believe.

Before this faith came, we were held prisoner by the law, locked up until faith should be revealed. So the law was put in charge to lead us to Christ that we might be justified by faith. Now that faith has come, we are no longer under the supervision of the law (Gal. 3:15-25).

Precious reader, with your destiny in your own hands, to make a critical decision based on the above facts, kindly ponder over the statement of either to be imprisoned by the law or to get your freedom through Jesus Christ. I would like, therefore, to encourage you to give your life to Christ for your freedom, for it is written, "If the son sets you free you shall be free indeed" (John 8:36). Again, "for the law of the spirit of life on Christ Jesus has set you free from the law of sin and of death" (Rom. 8:2).

The Resurrection Power of Jesus

The resurrection power of Jesus Christ is the very heart of Christianity because the apostle Paul reasoned and said, "And if Christ was not raised to life, our message is worthless, and so is your faith. If the dead won't be raised to life we have told lies about God by saying that he raised Christ to life, when he really did not. So if the dead won't be raised to life, Christ wasn't raised to life. Unless Christ was raised to life, your faith is useless and you are still living in sins. And those people who died after putting their faith in him are completely lost. If our hope in Christ is good only for this life, we are worse off than anyone else. But Christ has been raised to Life. And he makes us certain that others will also be raise to life" (1 Cor. 15:14-20).

The Qur'an has specifically confirmed about the death of Jesus Christ, who resurrected and ascended into Heaven. It is just amazing how the Qur'an could caution humanity not to doubt about Christ's resurrection power, for the Qur'an reveals,

So peace be on me on the day I was born and on the way I die; and may peace be upon me on the day I shall be raised to life. Such was Isa (Jesus) the son of Mariam (Mary) that is the whole truth which they still doubt. (Sura 19, Mariam 33-34)

Again, another Sura confirms this beyond any reasonable doubt, which states,

He said: "Isa (Jesus), I am about to cause your term on Earth to end and lift you up to Me. I shall take you away from those who disbelieve and exalt your followers above them till the Day of Resurrection. Then to Me you all shall return and I shall judge your disputes. As for those who disbelieved, they shall be sternly punished in this World and in the World to come; there shall be none to help them." (Sura 3, Al-Imran 55-56)

These two Suras from the Qur'an concerning the Lord Jesus Christ about His death and resurrection have really confirmed that Jesus is alive. It further explains that it was God who allowed Jesus to die in order to save mankind, to resurrect and to ascend into Heaven.

The Qur'an continues to caution by revealing, "That is the whole truth which they still doubt." In other words, the Qur'an has sounded a caution note to all and sundry not to lose sight of the fact that indeed the Lord Jesus died, resurrected, and ascended into Heaven.

The Gospel states that "when the morning was come, all the chief priest and elders of the people took counsel against Jesus to put him to death. And when they had bound him, they led him away and delivered him to Pontius Pilate, the governor. Then Judas, who had betrayed him, when he saw that he was condemned, repented and brought again the thirty pieces of silver to the chief priest and elders, saying that he had betrayed an innocent blood. And they said, "What is that to us? It is up to you." And he cast down the pieces of silver in the temple and went and hanged himself. The chief priest took the silver pieces and said, "It is not lawful to put them into the coffers because it is the price of blood." And they took counsel and bought three potter's field to bury strangers in (Matt. 27:1-7).

And it came to pass that Jesus stood before the governor, and the governor asked him, saying, "Are you the King of the Jew?" And Jesus answered and said, "You have said it." He was accused by the chief priest and elders, but he answered nothing. And it came to pass that there was a feast whereby one prisoner was set free. The governor brought Jesus and Barabbas before the people for them to choose one, but the chief priest and the elders persuaded the people that they should ask for Barabbas and destroy Jesus.

And it came to pass that when Pilate saw that he could prevail nothing but rather tumult was made, he took water and washed his hands before the multitude, saying, "I am innocent of the blood of this just person, you should see to it." Then answered all the people and said, "His blood be on us and our children."

After Barabbas had been released, the soldiers took Jesus into the common hall and gathered unto him the whole band of soldiers. And they stripped him naked and put on him a scarlet robe. And when they had plaited a crown of thorns they put it upon his head and reed in his right hand, they bowed the knee before him and mocked him, saying, "Hail, the King of the Jews." And they spat upon him and took the reed and smote his head. And after that they mocked him, they took the robe off him and put his own raiment on him and let him away to crucify him (Matt. 27:11-31).

And it came to pass that they crucified Jesus on the cross at Golgotha, meaning a place of skull. Jesus, when he had cried again with a loud voice, gave up the Ghost. And behold, the veil of the temple was rent in twain from top to bottom, and the earth did quake, and the rock rent. And the graves were opened, and many bodies of the saint, which slept, arose and came out of the graves after his resurrection and went into the holy city and appeared unto many. Now when the centurion and those that were with him watching Jesus saw the earth quake and those things that were done, they feared greatly, saying, "Truly this is the Son of God" (Matt. 37:50-54).

Joseph of Arimathea took the body and wrapped him in clean linen after he had obtained permission from Pontius Pilate. And he laid it in his own new tomb, which he had hewn out in a rock, and rolled a great stone to the door of the sepulcher and departed (Matt. 27:58-60).

Now on the day that followed the day of preparation, the chief priest and Pharisees came together unto Pilate, saying, "Sir, we remember what the deceiver said while he was yet alive. He said after three days, he will rise again. Command, therefore, that the sepulcher be made sure until the third day, or else his disciples will come in the night to steal him away and say unto the people, 'He is risen from the dead,' so that the last error shall be worse than the first."

Pilate said unto them, "You have your own watch, go your way and make it as sure as you can." So they went and made the sepulcher sure, sealing the stone and setting a watch (Matt. 27:60-66).

The greatest of all miracles happened on the first day of the week, for the Gospel declares,

> In the end of the Sabbath, as it has began to dawn towards the first day of the week, came Mary Magdalene and other Mary to see the sepulchre. And behold there was a great earth quake; for the angel of the Lord descended from Heaven and came and rolled back the back the stone from the door and sat upon it. His countenance was like lightning; and his raiment white as snow and for fear of him the keepers

did shake and became as dead men. (Matt. 28:1-4)

And the angel answered and said unto the women, "Fear not, for I know that you are looking for Jesus who was crucified. He is not here, for He is risen as He said, come and see the place where the Lord laid. And go quickly and tell His disciples that He is risen from the dead and behold He is gone before you unto Galilee, there shall you see Him. Lo, I have told you." And they departed quickly from the sepulchre with fear and great joy and did run to bring his disciples word, And as they went to tell his disciples behold, Jesus met them, saying, "All hail." And they came and held him by the feet and worshipped Him. Then Jesus said unto them, "Be not afraid, go and tell my brethren that they should go to Galilee and there shall they see me." (Matt. 28:5-10)

And it came to pass that after His resurrection, the Lord Jesus gathered His disciples and gave them assurance and commissioned them to spread the Gospel. Jesus said, "But you will receive power after the Holy Ghost has come upon you, and you shall be my witnesses on to Me, both in Jerusalem and Judea and in Samaria and unto the uttermost parts of the earth." And when he had spoken these things, behold, he was taken up, and a cloud received him out of their sight. And while they looked steadfastly toward heaven as he went up, behold, two men stood by them in white apparel, which also said, "You men of Galilee, why are you standing gazing up to Heaven? So shall he come in the same manner as you have seen him going" (Acts 1:8-11).

Above all, the prophet Isaiah, best described our Lord Jesus Christ, declares, "Surely he has borne our grieves and carried our sorrows, yet we did esteem him stricken, smitten of God and afflicted. But, He was wounded for our transgressions. He was bruised for our iniquities, the chastisement of our peace was upon

Him and with His stripes we are healed" (Isa. 53:4-5).

Dear reader, ponder over what Jesus said, "I am the resurrection and the life. He who believes in me will live, even though he dies" (John 11:25). Give your life to Him and have life.

The Second Coming of Christ

The Second Coming of Christ is preceded by a number of world-shaking events that will occur before Christ will return. Again, in Christian doctrine, the Second Coming of Christ is the anticipated return of Christ to rapture His followers. The Qur'an also supports the concept of the Second Coming of Christ, and it explicitly expresses itself that no one should doubt about this great upcoming event. The Qur'anic verse reveals,

> He was no more than a man whom We (God) favored and made an example to the children of Israel. Had it been Our will we could have replaced you with angels to succeed you on the earth. He (Jesus) is potent of the Hour of Doom. Have no doubt about (His) coming and follow Me. This is the right path; let the devil not mislead you, for he is your sworn enemy. (Sura 43, Al-Zukhruf 59-62)

The Qur'an has indicated clearly that Christ's return is

imminent and that is the right path; hence, nobody should doubt it. Christians and Muslims share the same views that Jesus Christ was raised to Heaven and will return to earth at the end times. However, both religions differ on how Christ will appear, but both teach that His return from Heaven will herald the climax of human history. The Second Coming of Jesus is drawing nearer and nearer because all the prophecies regarding the signs of the end times before Christ's return are fulfilling accurately. What is more? If both the Holy Bible and the Glorious Qu'ran have confirmed that Jesus Christ will return, then we are all reassured to prepare for the bridegroom. Above all, Jesus Christ had specifically and plainly on many occasion told us that He will come back to rapture His followers to Heaven. For Jesus said, "Let not your heart be troubled; you believe also in me. In my father's house there are many mansions, if it were not so, I would have told you. I am going there to prepare a place for you. I will come back and take you to be with me that you also may be where I am" (John 14:1-3).

This is great consolation that after Jesus comes back, there is going to be plenty of mansions in Heaven for everyone who is prepared. In other words, Heaven is large enough to accommodate everyone that wants to be saved, just like Christ's kingdom here on earth is large enough to accommodate every sinner that wants to be saved. In other words, Heaven is a prepared place for a prepared people.

The angels of God have said that the Lord Jesus will come back, and Jesus spoke to His disciples: "And he said unto them, 'It is not for you to know the times and seasons, which the father has put in his own power. But you shall receive power, after the Holy Ghost has come upon you: and you shall be witnesses unto me both in Jerusalem, and in all Judea, and Samaria and unto the uttermost part of the earth.' And when He had spoken these things, while they beheld, He was taken up, and a cloud received Him out of their sight. And while they looked steadfastly toward Heaven as He went up; behold two men stood by them in white apparel; which also said, 'You men of Galilee why do you stand gazing up to Heaven? This same Jesus, which is taking up from you into Heaven, shall so come in like manners as you have seen Him go into Heaven'" (Acts 1:7-11).

The Lord is going to come with His holy angels, and He is going to gather His elect from the four winds. St. Matthew states, "At that time the sign of the Son of Man will appear in the sky, and all the nations of the earth will mourn. They will see the Son of Man coming on the clouds of the sky, with power and great glory. And He will send His angels with a loud trumpets call, and they will gather His elect from the four winds, from one end of the Heavens to the other" (Matt. 24:30-31).

Again, the Gospel according to Matthew reveals, "For the son of Man is going to come in His father's glory with His angels, and then He will reward each person according to what he has done. I tell you the truth, some who are standing here will not taste death before they see the Son of Man coming in His Kingdom" (Matt. 16:27).

The Gospel has plainly declared that some people will not taste death before Jesus will appear in His glory, for it is written, "I tell you the truth, some who are standing will not taste death they see the Kingdom of God." Furthermore, the Gospel of Matthew has described how Jesus will appear. It states, "For as lightning that cometh from the East is visible even in the West, so will be the coming of the son of Man" (Matt. 24:27).

Christ is coming back not only to receive but to crown, for the epistle of Peter records, "And when the Chief Shepherd shall appear, you shall receive a crown of glory that faded not away" (1 Pet. 5:4).

The Gospel also encourages us to be patient for the coming of the Lord, for the general epistle of James tells us, "Be patient then, brothers, until the Lord's coming. See how the farmer waits for the land to yield its valuable crop and how patient he is for the autumn and spring rains. You too, be patient and stand firm, because the Lord's coming is near" (James 5:7-8).

The Second Coming of our Lord and Savior Jesus Christ is well known in the Christendom as the Blessed Hope. The Gospel reveals, "For the Grace of God that brings salvation has appeared to all men." Teaching us that denying ungodliness and worldly lusts, we should live soberly, righteously, and godly in this present world, looking for the Blessed Hope, and the glorious appearance of the Great God and our Savior Jesus Christ, who gave himself a peculiar people, zealous of good works. "These things speak, and exhort, and rebuke with all authority. Let no man despise thee" (Titus 2:11-15).

Finally, the epistle of Paul to the Thessalonians states, "For this we say unto you by the word of Lord, that we which are alive and remain unto the coming of the Lord shall not prevent them which are asleep. For the Lord shall descend from Heaven with a shout, with the voice of the Archangel and with the trump of God; and the dead in Christ shall rise first; then we which are alive and remains shall be caught together with them in the clouds, to meet the Lord in the air; and so shall we ever be with the Lord. Wherefore comfort one another with these words" (1 Thess. 4:15-18).

In other words, the Second Coming of Jesus Christ is therefore the hope of believers that God is in control of everything, for He is faithful in all His promises in His Word.

Dear reader, it is about time to prepare ourselves for the Second Coming of Jesus Christ. If Christ is coming to rapture His followers, where would be your stand, especially if you are not a Christian?

The Holy Spirit is the Power of God

The Holy Spirit is the means by which the Almighty God created the heavens and the earth. He is also the means by which creation is sustained at the present time. When God wants to use His Spirit on a special purpose, it is termed as the Holy Spirit. The Holy Spirit started His work since the beginning of creation. The Bible states, "In the beginning God created heaven and earth, and the world was without form and void and darkness was upon the face of the deep. And the Spirit of God moved upon the face of the waters" (Gen. 1:1-2). It will interest you to note that the Holy Spirit is being mentioned in the verses of the Qur'an.

The Sura records,

> To Musa (Moses) We (God) gave the scriptures and after him We (God) sent other messengers. We (God) gave Isa (Jesus), the son of Mariam (Mary), veritable

signs and strengthened Him with the Holy Spirit.
(Sura 2, Al-Baqara 87)

Again, another Sura also states,

We (God) gave Isa (Jesus), the Son of Mariam
(Mary), clear signs and strengthened Him with the
Holy Spirit. (Sura 2, Al-Baqara 253b)

These two verses: from the Qur'an have clearly stated how
Mary gave birth to Jesus by the power of the Holy Spirit and
whose ministry was full of signs and wonders. God used the Holy
Spirit to bring about the birth of Christ, for it is written, "She will
give birth to a son, and you are to give the name Jesus, because He
will save His people from their sins" (Matt. 1-21). What's more?
It is written pure and clear revealing the Holy Trinity in the verses
of the Qur'an and, for that matter, supporting the Christian
concept of the Triune God. The Holy Spirit has been mentioned
in the Qur'an several times, and many questions have been raised
about the identity of the Holy Spirit in the Qur'an. Many of the
questions come from Christians who wonder if the Holy Spirit
in the Qur'an is the third of the Trinity. On the other hand, the
Qur'an is very clear in denouncing the Trinity and affirming that
the Holy Spirit in the Qur'an is defined as the angel Gabriel
(Jebreel). However, the Christians, known as the People of the
Book, have the final word because they have clear proofs from
the scriptures to authenticate that the Holy Spirit is the third
of the Trinity and that the angel Gabriel is a messenger of God.
Therefore, the Qur'an, which is referred to as the "reminder to the
world" cannot overrule the fact that had already been established
since the foundations of the earth. Apparently, it was written in
the volumes of the Book because what is written is written, and
for that matter, no one can substitute one revelation for another
revelation.

The Lord Jesus Christ's full ministry began after the Holy

Spirit had come upon Him, for it is written, "Now when all people were baptized, it came to pass that Jesus also being baptized and praying the Heaven opened. And the Holy Spirit descended in a bodily shape like a dove upon Him and a voice came from Heaven which said, 'This is my beloved son, in Him I am well pleased'" (Luke 3:21-22). The Holy Spirit is here associated with power by which God was with Him, the power by which Jesus Christ performed mighty miracles during His early physical ministry. The Holy Spirit is the very presence of God's power actively working in His servants.

It came to pass that before the Pentecost, Jesus said, "And I will pray the father, and he will give you another counselor to be with you forever; even the spirit of truth; whom the world cannot receive, because it neither sees him nor knows him; you know him; for he dwells with you, and will be in you" (John 14:16-18). One thing that distinguishes true Christians from all other people in the world is that they have the Holy Spirit dwelling within them. For it is written, "It came to pass that the disciples assembled in Jerusalem, for the gospel reminds us that Peter and the disciples went to Jerusalem and went up into the upper room. They were with one accord in prayer and supplication, with the women, and Mary the mother of Jesus, and with his brethren" (Acts 1:13-114).

The Gospel declares, "When the day of Pentecost was fully come, they were with one accord in one place. And suddenly there came a sound from Heaven as of a rushing mighty wind, and it filled all the house where they were sitting. And there appeared unto them cloven tongue like a fire and sat upon each of them. And they were all filled with the Holy Ghost and began to speak with other tongues as the Spirit gave them utterance" (Acts 2:1-4).

After this wonderful experience, the Gospel tells us that Peter and the disciples began to spread the Gospel with all boldness, and they were confronted by the people in Judea. They accused them, saying, "These men are full of new wine." But Peter, standing up with the eleven, lifted up his voice and said unto them, "You men of Judea and all you that dwell at Jerusalem; be this known unto you and hearken to my words. For these are not drunken as you suppose, seeing it is but the third hour of the day. But this is that which was spoken by the Prophet Joel that "And it shall come to pass in the last days saith God, I will pour out of my Spirit upon all flesh; and your sons and daughters shall prophesy, and your young men shall see visions and your old men shall dream dreams. And on my servant and on my hand maidens I will pour out in those days of my Spirit and they shall prophesy" (Acts 2:13-18).

At the first outpouring of the Holy Spirit, men who had previously locked themselves into the upper room for fear of the Jews now confronted the Jews from all nations with the Gospel of Jesus Christ. After this, a new wave of fearful converts, who were the products of the previous outpouring of the Spirit, became emboldened by the second outpouring: "And when they had prayed the place was shaken where they were assembled together; and they were all filled with the Holy Ghost, and they spoke the word of God with boldness" (Acts 4:31).

Another demonstration of the Holy Spirit's power can be found in the resurrection of the Lord Jesus Christ. The resurrection of Jesus happened through the power of the Holy Spirit. Anyway, Jesus's own power and divinity could not be held by the claims of death, for just as He willingly gave up His life, He also had the power to take it back again. The father gave an official message that delivered Jesus from the grave, but yet Jesus was still raised by His own majesty and power because He had the right to come out of the grave. He knew that he had a divine power, and therefore, he had broken the chains of death, and He could no longer be held by them. But the actual power that raised His body was the power of the Holy Spirit. It was the power of the Holy Spirit by which the body of Jesus was raised from the grave after having laid there for three days and nights. For it is written, "Christ died for our sins once and for all, the righteous for the unrighteous, it bring to God. He was put to death in the body but made alive by the Spirit" (1 Pet. 3:18). Again, another further proof states, "If the spirit of Him who raised Jesus from the dead is living in you, he who raised Christ from the dead will also give life to your mortal bodies through His Spirit who lives in you." [Romans 8:11] Without the Holy Spirit, we would not know what sin is. With the Holy Spirit, we are able to see more clearly our own sinfulness in contrast to His holiness. He will bring us to our knees in surrender and deep humility, for it is written, "When the Spirit of truth comes, he will guide you into all the truth" (John 16:13).

The Holy Spirit convicts the world of sin, for our salvation begins initially with our being brought to a profound sense that we need a Savior. The Holy Spirit is the one who brings us to the realization of our need, for it is written, "And He, when He is come will convict the world in respect of sin, and of a righteousness, and of judgment of sin because they believe not on Me; of righteousness because I go to the Father, and ye behold Me no more, of judgment because the prince of this world have been judged" (John 16:8-11). The Holy Spirit is the only one who can convince men of sin.

Beloved, you can agree with me that when God spoke through the prophet Joel, "In the last days I will pour out my spirit upon all flesh," there is nothing that can annul it. Therefore, if you have not given your life to Christ, kindly do so and desire for spiritual gifts, for it belongs to everyone who is prepared.

Muslims are to Consult the Knowledgeable Christians for the Truth

The Glorious Qur'an refers to Christians and Jews as the People of the Book. The Qur'an, therefore, encourages the Muslims to search for the truth from the Christians and Jews. The Sura reveals,

> If you are in doubt of what We (God) have revealed to you, ask those who have read the Book before you. The truth has come to you from your Lord: Therefore do not be one of the doubters. Nor shall you deny the revelations of Allah, for then you shall be lost." (Sura 10, Yunus 94-95)

Again, another Sura bears testimony to the fact that Christians and Jews are called the People of the Book, which reveals,

> We have not sent any before you but men to whom
> We revealed Scriptures. Ask the knowledgeable
> Christians and Jews if you do not know. We sent them
> with clear proofs and Books. And we revealed to you
> the Reminder (Qur'an) so that you may make clear
> to men what has revealed to them, and that they may
> give thought. (Sura 16, Al-Nahl 43-44)

The above Qur'anic verses explicitly express that if Muslims are in doubt of the scriptures, they should not hesitate to consult the Christians and the Jews for the truth. According to the Qur'an, the Christians and the Jews were given clear proofs and books; therefore, the Qur'an refers to Christians and Jew as the People of the Book.

According to Christine Huda Dodge, the author of The Everything Understanding Islam Book, "Islam teaches that those of the Jewish or Christian faith are the 'People of the Book' meaning those who have received previous prophets and scriptures. Muslims respect the prophets of Judaism, Christianity and believes that the faiths share the original teachings."

She, therefore, quoted from the Qur'an to support her claims and stated, "Muslim are to speak to Jewish and Christian believers with words of respectful advice and try to find common ground. Islam teaches that Muslims should say, 'Oh! People of the Book! Come to common terms between us and you: That we worship none but God, that we associate no partners with Him, that we do not erect from among ourselves. Lords and patrons other than God'" (Qur'an 2:64). She further stressed that "Islam calls upon all people to engage in respectful dialogue, seeking the signs of God in the natural world and reflect on His message throughout the World."

Muslims are to consult the knowledgeable Christians and Jews when they are in doubt of the Torah (Old Testament) and the Injil (New Testament). Christian faith teaches that believers' doors are always open and that souls are always welcomed to come and know the truth. This kind of dialogue happened during Christ's ministry here on earth.

For instance, Nicodemus was a Pharisee and a member of the Sanhedrin. Apparently, Nicodemus was a wealthy person, educated, and a highly religious man in Israel. He was well respected by his people and apparently was a descendant of the patriarch Abraham. Jesus described Nicodemus as the teacher of Israel, implying that he was well trained in the Old Testament law and tradition. Jesus said to Nicodemus, "I tell you the truth no one can enter the Kingdom of God unless he is born of water and the Spirit, flesh gives birth to flesh but the Spirit gives birth to the Spirit you must be born again"

(John 3:5-7). In view of this wonderful experience, Nicodemus became a follower of Jesus Christ, and he, therefore, appeared in the Gospel three times following Jesus Christ. What is more? Nicodemus did not look at his position, neither did he rely on any material gains nor his religious background but humbled himself and came to Jesus by night in order to have eternal life.

Dear reader, as you are pondering over these words, to make a critical decision, I wish to present to you some of the declarations made by the (Truth) Jesus Christ of which no one else was able to make.

Jesus said,

> I am the light of the world, he that follows me shall
> not walk in darkness, but shall have the Light if life.
> (John 8:12)

> I am the bread of life. He who comes to me will never
> go hungry, and he who believes in Me will never thirst.
> (John 6:35)

> I am the door, if any one enters by me, he will be saved
> and will go in and out and find pasture. (John 10:9)

I am the true vine, and my Father is the gardener. Every branch in me that beareth not fruit he takes away and every branch that bears fruit, he purges it, that it may bring more fruit. (John 15:1-2)

I am the good shepherd, the good shepherd gives His life for the sheep. (John 10:11)

I am the resurrection and the Life. He who believes in me will live even though he dies. (John 11:25)

I tell you the truth, the man who does not enter the sheep pen by the gate, but climbs in by some other way, is a thief and a robber. (John 10:1)

That the thief does not come except to steal and to kill, and to destroy. I have come that they may have life, and have it more abundantly. (John 10:10)

Everyone who drinks the water will be thirsty again, but whoever drinks the water I give will never thirst. Indeed the water I give him will become a spring of water welling up to eternal life. (John 4:13-14)

To them again, most assuredly I say to you. I am the door of the sheep. All whoever came before me are thieves and robbers but the sheep did not hear them. (John 10:7-8)

Beloved, God is not a respecter of persons; and therefore, it is up to you to humble yourself and give your life to (the Truth) Jesus, for it is written, "You shall know the truth and the truth shall set you free" (John 8:3).

"Salvation": The Conceptual Views of the Bible, Qur'an, and other Religions

According to the Longman Dictionary of Contemporary English, salvation is "something that saves or preserves from danger, loss, ruin or failures." It went further to explain in the Christian context that salvation is "the state being saved from the power of evil." For instance, the salvation of the souls.

Again, the Expository Dictionary of New Testament Words defined salvation from the original Greek noun sonetra. Sonetra denotes deliverance and preservation. It goes on to explain that salvation means "material and temporal deliverance from danger and apprehension."

Furthermore, the Dictionary of the Bible tells us that salvation is "the generic term employed in scripture to express the idea of any gracious deliverance of God, but specially of the spiritual redemption from sin and its consequences predicted by the Old

Testament prophecies and realized in the mission of the Savior Jesus Christ."

Above all, in religion, salvation is the concept that God "saves" humanity from death as part of his plan to provide for them an eternal life. As commonly conceived, God has both the will and the means to realize human salvation, albeit through means regarded as mysterious and transcendent of current human understanding.

Drawing from the various definitions and authorities above, it is obvious that salvation, in its simplest term, means "providing deliverance," "an act of saving or salvation of the souls," and the like. It will interest you to know that a quotation from the Glorious Qur'an confirms the concept of salvation in Christianity.

The Sura reveals,

> Say, "I will pray to my Lord and associate none with him".

> Say, "I have no control over any good or evil that befalls you".

> Say, "None can protect me from Allah, nor can I find any refuge besides Him. My mission is only to make known His messages"; those that disobey Allah and His Apostle (Jesus) shall abide forever in the fire of Hell. (Sura 72, Al-Jinn 20-23)

This powerful message came through the prophet Mohammed (p.b.u.h.), which relates to a Christian doctrine and, for that matter, confirms God's plan of salvation He has provided for humanity. What's more? It has also revealed that the only way to escape hell fire is to believe in the Lord Jesus Christ. In other words, the only way one can get to Heaven is through Jesus Christ.

Having established that salvation can be attained or provided by a force beyond that of human power or by any supernatural power, it stands to reason that we can turn to the sacred writings of most of the religious groupings to ascertain what their inspired scriptures have to say about salvation. Let us now focus our attention on the salvation principle of Islamic religion.

> The weighing on that day is the true (weighing). As for those whose scale are heavy, they are successful. As for those whose scale are light: those are they who lose their souls because they disbelieved Our revelations. (Sura 7, Al-A'raf 8-9)

In Islam, there are two prominent ways to get to Paradise. If your good deeds outweigh your bad deeds, you will eventually get to paradise. Again, Muslims who die as martyrs by defending Islam will go directly to paradise. Salvation in Islam is attainable as a result of your good deeds. It will interest you to note that all Muslims, except those who die as martyrs by defending Islam, go through hell. This is clearly stated in the Qur'an: "There is not one among you who shall not pass through hell; such is the absolute decree of your Lord; We will deliver those who fear us and leave wrong doers there; on their knees" (Sura 19:70-72).

This Qu'ranic verse reveals that everyone goes through hell. After that, Allah will deliver those who have done enough good deeds and leave behind those who have not done enough good.

The Jewish Religion Says: "Moses writes of the righteousness of the law, whoever keeps it shall live by it."

The Hinduism Religion Says: Salvation for the Hindus is called Moksha. Moksha is when an enlightened human being is freed from cycle of life and death (the endless cycle of death and reincarnation) and comes into a state of completeness. He then becomes one with God.

The Buddhist Religion says: "Goodness and righteousness both are the road which leads to Nirvana—the greatest Good."

All these sayings are just fantastic, but they urge man to attain salvation by relying on works of the law; whereas in Christianity, it is a free gift from Jehovah God. It is like trying to squeeze water out of a stone, which is impossible. However, all these religious groupings' view points of salvation demand the impossibility of the individual. Consequently, there must be a way out that the individual can gain salvation without much difficulty. The prophet Isaiah rightly said, "All of us have become like one who is unclean, and all our righteous acts are like filthy rags; we all shrivel up like a leaf and like the wind our sins sweep us away" (Isa. 64:6).

Having established the above facts regarding the salvation principles from the various religious groupings, it is therefore significant to direct our attention to the Christian doctrine of salvation. The good news is that "Christ redeemed us from the curse of the law" (Gal. 3:13). Therefore, "For all who rely on works of the law are under curse; for it is written, Cursed be everyone who does not abide by all things written in the book of the law, and do them. Now it is evident that no man is justified before God by the law; for 'He who through faith is righteous shall live' but the law does not rest on faith, for 'He who does them shall live by them.' Christ redeemed us from the curse of the law, having become a curse for us—for it is written, 'Cursed be everyone who hangs on a tree'—that in Christ Jesus the blessing of Abraham might come upon the Gentiles, that we might receive the promise of the Spirit through faith"(Gal. 3:10-14).

When Jesus died on the cross for our sins, He took the curse upon Himself so that we could be free. If you believe and have faith that Jesus died for your sins, then you will be justified by faith. According to the book of the law, you either obey everything in the law perfectly or just break one and be under a curse. There is no in-between since it is impossible to live a perfect life and never sin; the only way to escape punishment from sin is to have faith in Jesus Christ, who already took our punishment for us.

The essence of the good news is that Jehovah God has

achieved eternal salvation for all who believe through the work of the sinless Son of God, Jesus Christ, who died on the cross of Calvary as the sin bearer of the world. In other words, God has rescued mankind through Jesus Christ, who died on the cross of Calvary. The Gospel records that the Son of man came to seek and to save those who are lost. God's salvation He had prepared for humanity was not an emergency one, but it was a preordained and a carefully worked-out plan. In order to achieve this objective, He prepared everything for salvation even to the extent of laying down His life for the sinner, impelled by the abundance of His love and mercy. The Bible records that our Lord's death was part of God's eternal decree, determined before creation, for it was written, "Knowing that you were not redeemed with perishable things like silver or gold from your future way of life inherited from your forefathers, but with precious blood, as of a lamb unblemished and spotless, the blood of Christ. For he was foreknown before the foundation of the world, but has appeared in these last times for the sake of you" (1 Pet. 1:18-20).

Christ's Substitutionary Sacrifice for Our Sins

Since the law was not able to deliver humanity from the power of sins and death, Jesus Christ, who is God, from Heaven became incarnate sharing in human flesh and blood in order to offer Himself as a substitutionary sacrifice for sin and thus destroying sin and breaking its hold on mankind. For it is written, "But when the fullness of time was come, God sent forth His son, made of a woman, made under the law, to redeem them that were under the law that we might receive the adoption of sons" (Gal. 4:4-5).

The substitutionary sacrifice of Christ on the cross satisfied for us all the claims of the law, which had brought curse on humanity, and by so doing fulfilled the prophetic words of the prophet Isaiah, who stated,

Surely he has born our griefs, and carried our sorrow; yet we did esteem him stricken, smitten of God and afflicted. But He was wounded for our transgressions, He was bruised for our iniquities, the chastisement of our peace was upon Him and with His stripes we are healed. All we like sheep have gone astray; we have turned everyone to his own way and the Lord has laid on Him the iniquity of us all. He was oppressed and he was afflicted, yet He opened not his mouth: He is brought as a lamb to the slaughter, and as a sheep before his shearers is dumb, so He opened not His mouth. He was taken from prison and from judgment: and who shall declare his generation; for He was cut off out of the land of the living; for the transgression of my people was he stricken. And he made his grave with the wicked, and with the rich in his death; because he had done no violence, neither was any deceit in his mouth. (Isa. 53:4-9)

That is why John the Baptist introduced our Lord Jesus by exclaiming, "Behold, the Lamb of God who takes away the sin of the world."

Dear reader, the gift is given to us freely and was made possible when Christ died and shed His blood at Calvary for our sins. By receiving Jesus Christ as your personal savior and Lord, trusting Him alone to save you, you can be born again. You can have eternal life today by faith in Jesus Christ. Romans 10:13 says, "For whosoever shall call upon the name of the Lord shall be saved."

Again, Romans 10:9 says, "If thou shall confess with thy mouth the Lord Jesus, and shall believe in thine heart that God has raised him from the dead thou shall be saved. For with the heart man believes on to righteousness and with the mouth confession is made on to salvation."

Dear friend, why not turn away from your sins right now and call upon the Lord to save your soul? Receive Jesus Christ as your Savior and serve Him faithfully until He returns.

At this juncture, you may be asking yourself this question, "What must I do to be saved?"

I will therefore ask you to take these necessary steps of salvation.

1. **ACKNOWLEDGE:** "For all have sinned and come short of the glory of God" (Rom. 3:23). You must acknowledge in the light of God's Word that you are a sinner.

2. **REPENT:** "Except ye repent ye shall likewise perish" (Luke 13:3). "Repent ye therefore, and be converted, that your sins may be blotted out" (Acts 3:19).

3. **CONFESS:** "If we confess our sins, He is faithful and just to forgive our sins, and cleanse us from all unrighteousness" (1 John 1:9).

4. **FORSAKE:** "Let the wicked forsake his way, and the unrighteous man his thoughts, and let him return unto the Lord . . . for He will abundantly pardon" (Isa. 53:7).

5. **BELIEVE:** "For God so loved the world that he gave his only begotten Son that whosever believeth in him should not perish, but have everlasting life" (John 3:16). "If thou shall confess with thy mouth the Lord Jesus, and shall believe in thine heart that God hath raised him from the dead thou shall be saved" (John 1:12).

6. **RECEIVE:** "But as many as received him, to them gave he power to become the sons of God, even to them that believe on his name" (John 1:12).

Dear precious reader, if you want to accept Jesus Christ as your personal Savior and Lord, it will help you to pray this prayer:

Dear Heavenly Father, I thank you for your dear Son, Jesus Christ, who came to die for my sins and to purify me from all unrighteousness by the power of His blood that was shed on the cross of Calvary.

I, therefore, ask your dear Son, Jesus Christ, to come into my heart this very moment, for it is written, "Behold I stand at the door and knock, if any man hears my voice and open the door, I will come in and eat with him and he with me" (Rev. 3:20).

I give you praises and honor due only to you. I will tell others of you and your dear Son, Jesus, so that they might also find abundant life. I thank you for answering my prayers, in Jesus's mighty name. Amen.

Dear reader, I wish to present to you some additional verses of salvation from the scriptures.

Neither is there salvation in any other; for there is none other name under Heaven given among men, whereby we must be saved (except through Jesus Christ). (Acts 4:12)

Believe in the Lord Jesus and you will be saved, you and your household. (Acts 16:31)

Repent, and be baptized, every one of you, in the name of Jesus Christ so that your sins may be forgiving, and you will receive the gift of the Holy Spirit. (Acts 2:38)

In Him we have redemption through His Blood the forgiveness of sins, in accordance with the riches of God's Grace. (Eph. 1:7)

But now in Christ Jesus you who once were far away

have been brought near through the Blood of Christ. (Eph. 2:13)

Conclusion

The Holy Bible and the Glorious Qur'an acknowledge the fact that Jesus Christ is the Messiah, the Word, and the Lord of all. Jesus Christ has therefore become the only one way to God's presence in Heaven. This is a proof that there is no other name given among men in which we should be saved, except through the name of Jesus Christ. In other words, there is no other way to get to Heaven except through Jesus Christ. The fact that the Bible and the Qur'an speak of the deity of Jesus Christ with the same passion reveals that He is the promised Messiah, who came to atone for our sins and reconciled us back to God. Those who are looking up to God for their salvation through other paths are doing so in their own condemnation.

I would therefore like to encourage you to choose the right way, who is Jesus Christ, the one and only way to the kingdom of God.

My Prayer

May God sanctify the Words in this book and guide all who are thirsty for the Truth to make the right decision. Amen.

Reader's Prayer

"Teach me your way; O Lord, and I will walk in your truth; give me an undivided heart, that I may fear your name" (Psalm 86:11). Amen.

Quiz Program

Dear reader,

If you read this religious book carefully, you can answer the following questions:

1. To whom was the law given? And who came with grace and truth?

2. Mention some of the events that characterized Christ's birth.

3. Which Qur'an verse calls on the Muslims to consult Christians for the true way?

4. Who came to prepare the way for Christ?

5. When Peter and his disciples were filled with the Holy Spirit, what happened next?

6. Which of the verses in the Bible and the Qur'an declares the Second Coming of Christ?

7. What does the Bible say about salvation?

8. What are the salvation principles of other religions?

9. Find out the declaration made by God concerning Jesus Christ.

10. What does the Bible say about those who observe the law?

11. Who redeemed us from the curse of the law?

12. What lessons can we draw from Nicodemus?

13. What was Apostle Paul's attitude toward the Galatians when they were observing the law?

14. Who does the Qur'an refer to as the People of the Book?

15. Can man of himself unaided by Christ keep the law, and why?

17. Who empowers Christ's followers to witness effectively for God?

18. Who is the Messiah? And what is its meaning?

19. Mention some of the events that characterized the resurrection of Christ.